John Swi. ____

OPEN VERDICT

This book is dedicated to my family who remind me every day that I can return to a normal life when I finish my shift. At least until my mobile phone rings!

I need to thank so many people for making this happen but especially Louise for inspiring me, Glenn for guiding me and Sue for believing in me.

Saturday, March 3rd 2007, 10PM

Something was wrong; he just couldn't put his finger on it. Ben Brown looked at the images again. The cover of the photograph album read:

"Unknown female   01.03.07   Bringholme Bay CSI Stitch"

Technically they were perfect; Mark Stitch was a good photographer, a complete arse, but a good photographer. Even so, something was very wrong with the photographs; Ben just couldn't work out what. On the face of it the scene photographs showed a simple suicide; a naked female washed up on the beach, not badly decomposed, with few obvious injuries but it just wasn't right. Why was she naked and weighted?

He reached for the scotch, the most essential tool in this CSI's box. God how he hated the term Crime Scene Investigator... Crime Scene Imbeciles as far as he was concerned. CSI was a fine example of the corrupting power of television... Ben was a SOCO not a CSI. A good old fashioned Scenes of Crime Officer who worked away from the limelight using physical evidence to solve crime.

The French scientist Edmund Locard had said way back in 1910 when writing the theory on which all of modern forensic science was based:

"Every contact leaves a trace ... Whatever you do, wherever you go, you will leave some physical evidence behind and take some physical evidence away with you"

This statement was as true now as it had ever been and physical evidence needed careful examination rather than showy, headline grabbing CSI style gimmicks. Stitch was a show off CSI through and through but it had to be admitted, he was also a good photographer so Ben took another reassuring mouthful of whiskey and looked again at the images before him.

5 feet 10 or there abouts. She was not fat but not slim either. She had blonde shoulder length hair (well at least the bit that was left). Looking lower down it seemed she was a natural blonde as well,

"It doesn't look as though she was attractive, even before she died and got eaten by crabs. Her face is a bit too hard and her shoulders a touch too broad. No reason to top yourself though." He thought.

He wondered, not for the first time, what constituted 'a reason'? When does life get that bad that it is time to end it? And why is it so hard to tell anyone that you have reached such a point?

"So, you have had enough and decide to go for that final swim. You want to make sure you don't make it back to shore so you weigh yourself down. You carry the weights don't you, or you fill your pockets. The wet clothes will help drag you down. Why strip them off then?"

Another mouthful, Louisa had always moaned about his drinking. She had often told him she had two rivals, his job and his bottle and she felt she couldn't compete with either. Ben closed his eyes and saw Louisa in that green dress she had always looked so good in, but the image hurt too much, so he quickly opened them again and with slightly trembling hands picked the scene photographs up once more.

"Right, until we know who you are I'll call you Sandy".

Yes, he knew it was in very poor taste but you couldn't do this job for long without either getting very hard hearted or going mad... which was he? He felt that the most honest answer was probably a bit of both.

Photograph seven was actually a very good photograph; it could easily win an award if 'Practical Photographer' had a "Best Naked Dead Person" category in its annual competition. It was taken from close to the lower left foot and showed Sandy lying on her back, her legs slightly apart, her arms splayed out, looking like some giant, bizarre, alien starfish. The two weights were the type that they used to have on parcel scales in railway stations, big square iron blocks with handles forged into them. One weight was lying on either side of the body and the chain went through the handles, passed around Sandy's neck and then down between her legs and round the left leg where it was fastened with a padlock. She was lying on the strand line, the place where the high tide dumps seaweed, driftwood and, apparently, dead bodies. She was positioned with her head towards the shore. The cliffs were visible behind her, their outlines clearly highlighted by the light from the setting sun. Yes it was a very good photograph.

Was it the chains that were causing Ben to feel so ill at ease? Over clothes they would be uncomfortable, but naked... Surely no matter how painful waxing was, it had to be preferable to pulling hairs out this way. Yes, the chains formed part of his unease but there was something else, something he was missing. After all he had seen other, far stranger, swimmers in the past.

He closed his eyes again, remembering one of the strangest he had encountered in his career....

The Cycle of Life

I walked down the quayside of Bringholme's West Dock, the older, more commercial part of the harbour, striding purposefully past half a dozen semi derelict trawlers that appeared not to have been out to sea for a long while (the European Union does not think about the terrible pain, caused to individual skippers, in order to maintain the greater good by imposing quotas on fishing activity). The dark portholes of each one looked like the dead eyes of some giant metal skeleton. Scattered amongst them were a couple of newer looking rig support vessels, with generators thrumming and lights blazing in their bridges, galleys and crew cabins. I continued briskly on, until I reached pontoon number 4E where the moored lifeboat was rocking gently amongst the empty drinks bottles, dead fish and other usual rubbish found in the oily waters of a working harbour. John, the coxswain, was waiting for me.

"Welcome aboard Ben, you haven't been out on this beauty yet have you? It's one of the new Severn class boats, goes like shit off a shovel, though it does tend to bounce around a bit... er sorry, I forgot" he said with his grin widening as he spoke "you aren't very keen on these trips are you? Never mind though the 'Mirabelle' is only about a mile offshore so it shouldn't take us long to reach her. Normally of course we would just take a couple of snaps ourselves, bloody good things these digital cameras but when the coastguard told me what the Mirabelle had caught I thought I had better offer you a ride…. Here pass up your cases and put this on, have you got a body bag or do you want to use one of ours? By the way did you bring the bolt croppers?"

A few pleasantries later I was safely in a reassuringly sturdy lifejacket, sitting in the cockpit of the lifeboat with the crew and we were on our way. John had been right on both counts; it did 'go like shit off a shovel' and couldn't exactly be described as a comfortable ride. Thankfully for my stomach the ride was as short as he had suggested and I was soon being helped aboard the 'Mirabelle'. She... Why are all boats female anyway?...was a small fishing vessel and had the usual smell of diesel oil and fish guts but Mirabelle's perfume had been blended with 'Eau de Rotting Corpse'. This was one of those instantly recognisable smells that you get used to in this job. The body was on the deck next to a large hatch leading to the fish storage area. The captain looked exactly like Captain Birdseye but without the smile. I thought it best not to point this out to him though, as he seemed like the sort of person who might just enjoy keel hauling me.

"If I'd known it would cause all this fuss I'd have thrown the bugger back in, are you going to be long 'cause I've got a living to make?"

I assured Captain Grindle that I would not be long and started work, The body was male, middle aged, wearing grey trainers, blue jeans and a black 'T' shirt that proclaimed, in big white letters across the chest

A B C

D E F

U C K

O F F

He was clean shaven and fairly stocky with dark brown hair and a bald patch. His eyes had been eaten away, presumably by crabs, as had part of his nose and one of the fingers of his left hand. He was extremely bloated, his skin had developed a soapy texture due to decomposition and, somewhat unusually for a body found floating a mile off shore, his right hand was handcuffed to the handlebars of a dark blue 'Europa' mountain bike which was in gear five. The front tyre was flat but of course that could have been due to the crabs as well.

Working alone and as quickly as I safely could I photographed him from all angles after which I carefully cut through the handcuff chain. Then, only holding the pedals, and wearing gloves so as to lessen the chance of damaging any evidence from potential offenders I passed the bike across the narrow but perilous gap to the crew of the waiting lifeboat. The gloves were the only "forensic protection" I wore, having decided that full personal protective equipment in this situation posed too much of a health and safety risk.

Later, once safely back on dry land I would carry out a fingerprint examination on the bike and handcuffs using something called Small Particle Reagent which is ideal for examining things that have been wet, such as push bikes recovered from the North Sea. Next I bagged the dead man's head and hands in grip seal bags to prevent evidence falling off. Though this seemed like overkill bearing in mind the circumstances of the find, any evidence was now most likely sprinkled over several tonnes of cod on its way to your table… Nice!

I then placed the entire body in the sterile body bag that I had 'borrowed' from John, zipped it up and with the help of a couple of friendly lifeboatmen transferred it across the small stretch of water between the two boats and reunited it with its pushbike.

The following morning found me at the post mortem examination of the man from the 'Mirabelle' taking yet more photographs, removing and exhibiting his clothing, packaging samples from him such as his blood, hair, and stomach contents…

"What did you do at work today?"

"Nothing exciting, just bagged up some dead mans sick"

… and collecting impressions of his fingerprints. This activity was complicated by the degree to which he was decomposed. Immersion for a long time in water causes the top layer of skin, the epidermis, to start to peel away from the lower levels causing any attempts to get a likeness using ink to end up producing a smudgy mess with bits of skin sticking to it. The solution to this problem that I chose involved carefully cutting the top layer of skin away from the lower layers using a scalpel, then placing the removed, dead finger skin over my gloved fingers before inking and printing them then reuniting them with the rest of the body

Later, results from the toxicology samples taken from the body would show that he   had fatal levels of paracetamol and antidepressant drugs in his system. Identification of the fingerprints I had taken from him showed him to be a suicidal missing person, Duncan Longhorn, who had worked as a deck hand on "Lady Isabelle", one of the rusting trawlers I had passed on the dockside as I walked to the lifeboat prior to meeting him. Duncan had not found it easy to adapt to life on the dole when The Lady was moored up for her last time. His depression had deepened when his wife Clare declared that she could not stand living with him any more "because of him being a big black cloud hanging over her and the house". He had been prescribed antidepressants but did not take them regularly, as he should have. He had talked of suicide, to his few remaining friends, in the days leading up to his disappearance, although no note was found when his house was searched.

His fingerprints were the only ones found on the pushbike. I concluded that the most likely explanation for his death was that he had taken an overdose, locked himself to his pushbike and cycled quickly along Bringholme pier, though I suppose it could always have been a disastrous wrong turn whilst out for his Sunday morning bike ride...

Saturday, March 3rd 2007, 10.01PM

Smiling at this final thought, Ben opened his eyes and looked again at the photograph in his hand. If you could explain away handcuffing yourself to a pushbike and going for a swim, the chains wrapped around Sandy could be explained far more easily. Even given the fact that she was naked. No, the problem was not the chains. Something, however, was still very wrong.

Never mind. Tomorrow should see the results from the fingerprints Ben had taken from Sandy's body. Her fingerprints were the reason that Ben had got involved with this case in the first place. You see, the thing about Stitch was this. Despite his applied forensic measurement degree, when it came to fingerprinting decomposed bodies he was crap. Ben on the other hand had no degree but did have a few old tricks up his sleeve.

Photographs 12 and 13 were close up shots of her hands. Both hands were quite badly damaged due to their extended wash in salt water but the right hand had also been burnt quite severely. He might not have a fancy forensic degree but Ben was pretty damn sure that this injury had not occurred during Sandy's last swim. So how had the burn been caused and in what way was it significant? You don't top yourself just because you have burnt your hand... unless of course someone had burnt it for you and the burn was your final straw. Was it possible that, abused beyond belief and believing there was no hope of escape; she took her life by stripping off and walking out to sea carrying 30 pounds of iron in her hands? Her burnt hands? It was possible, yes, but not very likely, and besides, if she had been abused, where were all her other injuries? She was naked for God's sake. Abusers don't like to leave marks where they can be seen by friends and neighbours, so it was not surprising that there were no injuries to Sandy's face. A burnt hand could be explained away to nosey busy bodies but surely there should be some decent bruising to places such as the tops of her legs and arms and of course to her belly, the safe places to injure someone without it being noticed.

Sorry but the 'abused wife finally ends it all by drowning herself' theory just didn't hold water. Ben smiled at this. He really had missed his true vocation as a comedian.

Thinking about water and burning at the same time brought to mind a case he had dealt with a few years previously. That particular case had ended in an open verdict. You get those when the coroner can't decide if the death was an accident or a suicide. Or sometimes when he has decided which, but feels it is kinder for the relatives to be able to go on believing that someone's death could have (but in truth probably hadn't) happened by accident. Ben knew all about the 'kindness' of open verdicts didn't he? He felt his chest tightening and a lump forming in his throat. He forced these feelings back deep within him, forced himself not to think about the open verdict in relation to Louisa's death but to think instead of the circumstances surrounding the death that he had investigated a few years ago. Would there be anything he could take from that case and use to help him make sense of Sandy's arrival on the beach at Bringholme Bay.

Don't Let the Bath Go Cold

The house was an unremarkable right hand semi which appeared to have been built in the 1930's. Its neat outline with bow windows to the front had been spoiled at some point in its history by the addition of grey stone cladding but the inside was tastefully decorated in a modern, fairly minimalist style with cream carpets and dark brown leather furniture. Abstract, original modern artwork hung on most walls. The kitchen had a genuine grey marble work surface, separated from the tiled floor by light oak units, with the cooker, fridge and washing machine being stainless steel to match the pots, pans, kettle and toaster. Everything was spotlessly clean and tidy.

Although it was the middle of January and the ground outside wore a hard white frost which had not lifted in spite of the best efforts of the weak, mid-day sun, hanging in a sky so blue that it looked as though you could jump up and go for a swim in it, the house was almost unbearably hot and stuffy. Like the atmosphere in a greenhouse in mid-July with the door shut, or like a school kitchen just before noon. The hooded white paper suit and facemask didn't help matters and the mask, whilst admirably doing its job of stopping the scene being contaminated by any of my DNA, was failing miserably to protect me from the overpowering stench. This was an aroma that even I was not completely familiar with. It can be best described as a cross between the coppery blood smell in the slaughter room of an abattoir and an over cooked Sunday roast dripping with slowly hardening white fat.

The thing that people who are lucky enough not to have to wear them, don't realise about forensic facemasks is that they feel really claustrophobic and make your nose sweat and run awfully, and of course you cannot wipe your nose as that defeats the object of wearing the mask in the first place. Ben snot all over a crime scene would not be good. One of the most irritating things about programmes like CSI is that the characters always manage to look glamorous in a scene suit, that is, on the rare occasions that they bother to wear one. This simply just does not happen in real life, the terms "glamorous" and "overgrown, white paper baby grows" just do not go together.

The source of the unpleasant smell, I quickly discovered, was Mrs Irene Taylor. I am sure that she smelt beautiful when she was alive, and judging by the wedding photo in the lounge she had, in her younger days, been an attractive lady as well, about 5 feet 6 inches tall with jet black, shoulder length hair, green/grey eyes and a slim figure. But now, several years after the photograph had been taken, and having lain in a bath for a few days sharing it with a ceramic heater she didn't look, or smell, her best. Modern electrical appliances and domestic wiring circuits are designed with safety as a top priority. If you drop a heater into a bath for instance, the power should go off immediately thus preventing you from being fried. Something, however, had gone horribly wrong in this case. The open verdict eventually recorded was because no one could be sure that Irene Taylor had intended killing herself. Sure, there was an almost empty bottle of wine on the edge of the bath and an electric fire sharing the bath with her but as far as anyone knew Mrs Taylor was not depressed and hey, who doesn't drink in the bath eh? As for the fire, everyone knows that you should not have electrical items in a bathroom but then again, it would have been cold in there at this time of year. Whilst the house was centrally heated, there was no radiator or other safe form of heating in the bathroom.

The important question in this case was how had the fire ended up in the bath with Irene, rather than remaining relatively safely on the floor by the toilet? As I saw things, there were three possibilities, accident, suicide or murder. Considering them one at a time my thinking went like this: Possibility one. The heater had two heat settings (it was set to low when found in the bath) and Mrs Taylor had drunk almost an entire bottle of wine, not thinking straight due to the alcohol she could have reached over the edge of the bath to pick up the heater and turn it up or down. The heater could easily have slipped from her wet hands and joined her in the bath.

The second possibility of course was that Irene was terribly, terribly sad but had managed to keep this fact from her family and friends. She was an intelligent lady, having been a primary school teacher before she died, and would have known that electricity and water do not mix .It was entirely possible that Mrs Taylor had drunk her wine, said goodbye to the world that she felt had treated her so cruelly and picked up the heater....

If this is what had happened, what she, or no one else could have envisaged was the particular combination of faults, both on the heater and the house wiring which meant that the heater did not fail on contact with the water as it was designed to do but merely acted like the element in a kettle. Mrs Taylor was electrocuted, and hopefully died almost instantly, but then the temperature of her bath water gradually started to rise....

A not uncommon kitchen appliance is a slow cooker, a pot which you fill with meat and vegetables and a bit of stock and leave to slowly cook over the course of a day. The meat ends up really tender and simply falls off the bones. Well, Mrs Taylor's homemade slow cooker worked nearly as well, considering that she was a little larger than the average chicken joint. It did of course take quite a bit longer to cook her and by that time the parts of her that were not covered by the water had started to decompose. It was that mixture of slow cooked and rotting flesh that had caused the novel aroma I had noticed, despite my facemask, when I entered the house.

I considered the third possibility .Had someone murdered Irene? This was very unlikely. There was no Mr Taylor; he had died of lung cancer a couple of years previously. Mrs Taylor lived a simple solitary life with no one having any apparent reason to want to kill her. The house had been secure until the police forced the kitchen door to gain entry. They had been called because her neighbours were concerned that they had not seen Irene for several days and her post and milk was beginning to stack up. The only fingerprints I found on the wine bottle, the bath, extension lead and plug etc. matched the impressions I had taken from Mrs Taylor's, cooked and rotting body during the post mortem examination that was carried out on her. The neatly tiled bathroom floor bore no footprints other than hers. I was completely satisfied that Irene Taylor was the only person present in the house at the time of her death. I could rule out possibility three, but as for the first two; both scenarios were equally likely based on the evidence available to me. Yes, in this particular case an open verdict had been the correct one as far as I was concerned.

Sunday, March 4th 2007, 1.23 AM

"I should write a story about some of the shit I come across" thought Ben as he lay awake, yet again unable to sleep because of the dark tangled mass of tumbleweed thoughts blowing about his head. "It would make me a million if only I could string two words together; I bet Mr "Degree Boy" Stitch could write a story, hell, he could write a whole bloody movie script."

What are the chances of the job involving Sandy ending with an open verdict wondered Ben. Not high. Sure, the weights and chains could have been put in place by Sandy herself but it just did not seem likely. He decided that there was no way, tonight, that he could beat the insomnia which seemed to get more aggressive with each passing night since Louisa's... well, since he had become a bachelor again. So he got out of bed, went through to the lounge, sat down in his 'thinking chair' and picked up Dr Hopton's post mortem report. Scanning through the pages he absorbed the important points.

"Female... 5feet nine inches tall" How good am I, one inch out from just looking at a photo thought Ben "medium build ... well nourished... blond shoulder length hair... brown eyes ... minimal dental work... mid-twenties ...tattoo on the lower back depicting a phoenix and flames".

With that description you would have thought she would have been flagged up by FIND, the Facial Image National Database, a collection of digital images of offenders and missing persons.

"No obvious trauma apart from a burn to the right palm and fingers... no signs of recent sexual activity" Not a surprise really as she has been in the sea for a while, or perhaps she just had crabs. Yes, thought Ben I really should be a comedian. "Internal examination shows full hysterectomy and appendectomy, organs NAD (no abnormalities detected)... small amount of water in lungs.... Cause of death; saltwater drowning".

Ben wondered about the post mortem report. Could the pathologist have gotten it wrong? Instinct told him that there was something about Sandy that everyone was missing. Ben had the uncomfortable thought that whilst Dr Hopton was a well-respected Home Office pathologist, even top class pathologists sometimes make mistakes. What was wrong? He decided to go through the facts of this case once more, one bit at a time starting at the beginning. Ben picked up the scene photos again, wondering even as he did so why he was bothering. It was the early hours of the morning and he was at home. It wasn't even his case and he was damn sure that super boy Stitch would not be worrying about it. He would be wowing some poor unsuspecting girl in some club somewhere, by telling her all about being the best CSI in the country. Still, Ben couldn't sleep anyway so he may as well try and answer some of the questions that were haunting him.

Who are you Sandy?

Where did you come from?

Where did you go swimming?

Did you walk in or were you thrown in?

Where are your clothes?

Is there a car somewhere?

Where did you get the chain and weights?

Why use the weights?.... Why use the weights? Is that the key question ...why use the weights? He allowed his eyes to close and his mind to replay the scene of a previous murder where weights may just have helped.

Come In, the Water is Lovely

Most people believe that dead bodies sink when placed in water, they are wrong. What normally happens is the body lays face down on the surface of the water for a while, and then the feet sink, slowly, so that for a time the body appears to be 'treading water'. Then the body gracefully sinks to the bottom, where it lays until decomposition causes gasses to form, in the gut first. These gasses cause the body to slowly rise back to the surface after a few days. This mistaken belief that bodies sink, means that only rarely do people who are disposing of bodies, bother to weigh them down. Suicides on the other hand will often carry weights or fill their pockets with stones in order to overcome their natural instinct to swim to safety.

As I trudged across the muddy field, towards the small crowd of people gathered about 100 yards away, there was little sign that this was a murder scene. Yes, I had passed through a taped off cordon at the gateway. But normally when I enter a scene, I can see a body and normally there is no-one else in there with me. In this case I could see no corpse but I could, through the morning mist, see six people standing in a huddle. One of these people was rather bizarrely wearing a diver's dry suit, mask and air tank and appeared to be talking to the floor.

When I eventually reached the small gathering, with my feet beginning to feel cold in the Wellington boots, that now felt at least three times as heavy as when I had put them on, it all became a bit clearer. Mister Dry Suit was not talking to the floor. He was talking through a manhole cover in the concrete pad on which we were now all standing, to a similarly dressed colleague who was floating in a tank, about fifteen feet in diameter, which he was sharing with two decomposed corpses. After I had taken a few initial photographs, a plan was devised to allow the safe removal of the bodies through the small opening. Once they were safely above ground, the Pathologist and I were able to make a closer inspection of the two latest additions to our 'Foggy Field Gang' and I was able to take some further photographs.

The couple (and indeed it turned out that they were a couple) consisted of a slim dark haired girl dressed in a light blue skirt, white 'belly top' and one high heeled black shoe. She appeared to probably be in her late teens or early twenties and had almost certainly been quite pretty, but a couple of weeks immersion had seriously spoiled her looks. Her partner was older. A stocky man with short cropped ginger hair and a goatee beard. He was dressed for the outdoors, wearing brown 'Cat' work boots, faded and worn blue jeans and a cheap wax jacket. (You could tell it was a cheap version of the famous 'Barbour jacket' as it had far less pockets). It appeared at first sight to be the scene of a suicide pact but something was wrong with that theory. If it was a suicide pact, why was he nowhere near as decomposed as she was?

Later that day, I found myself in the mortuary holding hands with dead bodies again. Subsequent identification of the fingerprint impressions I had taken from the corpses, showed them to be a couple who had endured a stormy relationship, to say the least. The results of the post mortem examinations showed that she had died of strangulation and he had drowned. Could this, then, be a murder followed by the suicide of the killer?

"Racked with guilt for strangling his girlfriend, the killer had dived into the murky water to be with her again." This theory also did not sit comfortably with me, due to the fact that he had died a week after she had her last breath squeezed out of her. Also, murderers who feel that guilty that they decide to end their lives seem to have a tendency to decide to confess to their crime at the same time. There was no note or other indication that suicide had been on the menu.

So what had really happened in that tank, and why? No one alive will ever know for sure, but my best guess is this. James and Laura, for those were the names of the couple, had lived in a village about two miles from the scene. James was a farm worker and the tank in which they were found was on the land he worked. This tank was, for want of a better description, a large 'well' designed to provide some of the farm's water supply. On the night of Laura's murder, James and Laura went out for the evening and either on the way home, or soon after they got home, an argument started. Probably because Laura had spoken to another man. After all she was very pretty and lots of blokes fancied her. This was a problem as she had an insanely jealous boyfriend. During this argument James strangled her with his bare hands, using enough force to break the hyoid cartilage (voice box) in her neck. Keeping the pressure there, until her delicate hands stopped trying to pull his rough farmers hands from her neck, and her slight frame went limp.   James then decided, rather than owning up to his crime, to dispose of the body down the well in the field behind Jackson's barn. Believing no doubt that Laura would simply sink and remain hidden forever. We learnt from enquiries made locally that he had told his friends, she had 'gone away for a few days', at about the time she disappeared. For some reason, about a week later, he returned to the well. Perhaps out of morbid curiosity, or merely to confirm that she really had gone. It must have been a bit of a shock, after he had lifted the heavy iron manhole cover, to see Laura's now bloated, decaying face smiling up at him from the surface of the water, about four feet below him. Perhaps he thought he could reach through the hole, and either push her back under the water again, or pull her out to hide her elsewhere. Whatever the motive for his actions, the unexpected result of them was that he somehow toppled in next to her. The opening must have been tantalisingly close, but just out of reach, as he clawed at the walls and frantically trod water, getting gradually colder and weaker, whilst all the time trying not to look at his dead girlfriend, floating gracefully next to him.

Sunday, March 4th 2007, 1.34 AM

"Dead girlfriend… No don't go there", Ben told himself. He looked again at the photographs in his hand. It was almost as though the answer was calling to him. The answer or at least the path to the answer lay in these photographs. But where? Ben thought of one of those 3D pictures, the sort where if you slightly crossed your eyes, a hidden image appeared. There was something hidden in these photographs as well, but he didn't need to cross his eyes to find it. On the contrary he needed to look very, very hard.

Sunday, March 4th 2007, 1.57 AM

It suddenly struck him with such force, that he almost laughed out loud thinking about everyone's blindness, including his own. He did not laugh though, instead he said softly under his breath

"Hypostasis. Sandy, you have got hypostasis. You poor cow, you didn't want to die did you …. But someone else wanted you dead, and made sure it happened"

He got up and made his way back to bed, sure that for now at least he would be able to fight off his sleeplessness. He would let Superintendent Smith, and the incredibly stupid Stitch know in the morning.

Sunday, March 4th 2007, 8.11 AM

"Late again, big Ben". Mark Stitch was sitting with his feet on the edge of his desk, with his chair rocked back onto its two back legs. He had his hands folded behind his head, and a smug look on his face. Ben suppressed an urge to go over, and give Stitch a well-deserved lesson about how it felt to wear a black eye. Instead, he contented himself by imagining how good he would feel, if Stitch was to lean just a fraction too far backwards. Ben walked over to his own desk, without a word, and turned on his computer, entering the three random number passwords necessary to log him onto the secure police system.

"Grieves wants to see you." Referring to Detective Inspector Lee Grieves. "Didn't seem very happy, have you been upsetting the punters again? By telling them that if they had locked their door, they wouldn't have had their stereo nicked. By the way, I've solved the bird on the beach job, gonna tell Smith about it when he comes in. You can come along too, big Ben. Watch and learn my man, watch and learn."

Ben's heart sank; he couldn't believe that Stitch was once again going to steal the glory.

"Sorry" he said "While you are knocking the boss out with your shear brilliance, some of us have work to do." He continued, looking at his computer screen" I see that overnight three units on the Willow estate have been screwed. I had better pop down and throw some dust around, you never know, I might just get lucky. I see Brian Hales is back out of prison, they're just perfect for one of his jobs, and we both know that whenever he is pissed up, he forgets to wear gloves"

Ben got up and walked across the office to the evidence examination room, set off to one side, behind a part glazed door. As he filled the kettle and put it on, he called back.

"Come on then Sherlock; let's hear how you solved it"

Listening to Stitch's wild theory, about Sandy's death being the result of a sex game gone wrong, Ben almost laughed out loud. Ben had seen several auto erotic asphyxiation cases over the years. He felt that the habit of partially suffocating yourself, in order to gain sexual pleasure, was both pointless and stupidly dangerous. Though to be fair, it wasn't something he had ever been tempted to try, so perhaps, he thought, he was not the best person to judge…. Leave that to the experts. He was sure it was something that Stitch probably knew only too well.

As Stitch started to explain in detail, how the weights would pull the chain against the back of the girl's neck, Ben's mind began to wander to his least favourite case ever. A case involving auto erotic asphyxiation and one which he would have willingly passed over to Stitch, had he known……

Anyone for Guinness

It was a Saturday evening in September 2003, unusually warm, as Britain was in the 'Indian summer' that followed the killer heat wave of the true summer. I parked my SOCO van next to the panda car in the car park at Holme point. (am I the only person left alive who calls them panda cars? After all, they don't look very much like pandas anymore, now that they are covered in reflective green checkerboard markings). Having loaded myself up with my camera case, my general scene case and a body bag, I started down the steep and winding path through the trees. The sun was starting to set and the mosquitoes were beginning to bite, not that I was in a position to swat them, considering how heavily laden down I was. By the time I had reached the police tape marking the edge of the cordon, I was sweating profusely. I had left the main path a minute or so earlier, and travelled along a 'path' that was merely a worn down walkthrough, amongst the gorse and scrubby trees.

Detective Constable Constable (I couldn't help thinking anyone who joins the police, when they have the surname 'Constable', must have a wicked sense of humour) briefed me as to the facts known so far.

"Two young lads found him, playing hide and seek they were, one went to hide under that tree there" he pointed to a small but dense tree, more of a large bush really, over to my left. There was an opening through the branches at ground level on the side facing us, probably originally formed by animals, badgers perhaps, pushing through. "and found a pair of legs looking at him from inside the tree. We were called and Ian Rudge was first on the scene. Mind that sick over there" he pointed again "that's Ian's, I've sent him back to get cleaned up. From what he said, it looks like the guy's hung himself. Apparently he's a bit of a mess, though I haven't looked myself. That's your job old boy; give me a shout when you are done"

I unpacked my Bronica 645 medium format camera, and Metz flash from the case. (We didn't go digital till that December, and what a lovely Christmas present that was) I picked up my torch, as it was now starting to get quite dark, and would be darker still under the canopy of autumn leaves. Kneeling down I crawled through the opening. The 'inside' of the tree was like a large garden umbrella, which had started to shut down on top of me.

My feeling of claustrophobia increased when I looked up to see who I was sharing my 'den' with. Brian Jameson had been a big man in most respects. He was about six feet two inches tall and weighed a little over fifteen stone. I could not help feeling that I was not seeing his best side. This was probably true, considering I was kneeling between his legs, his naked legs, due to the fact that his trousers were round his ankles. And I was looking up at him with his naked, still erect, though slightly mouldy, member clasped in his hand a few inches above my face. My first thought, after, of course, "ugh that's gross" was "He cannot be dead, because he is being sick over me". A millisecond later I realised that the slow stream of white lumps, dropping from his mouth and nose, and landing all over my head, shoulders and expensive camera equipment was not vomit as I had first thought, but maggots that had been disturbed from their quiet feeding frenzy, by my rude entry into their world. A quick evaluation of the scene, told me that there was going to be no way that I was going to stand next to him and take any photographs. There simply was not room for two in this particular tree. I considered my options. Resigning there and then, and going off to get very drunk, seemed to be my favourite, but I had a mortgage to pay, so decided on option two instead. Option two involved rolling over so that I was lying on my back looking up at Brian (Though at that stage we had not been formally introduced, so I thought of him as "the body"). Raising the eyepiece of my Bronica to my left eye, I adjusted the focussing ring, and shifted my position slightly, until I had Brian framed correctly and looking nice and sharp, well sharp at least, as he looked far from nice in his current condition. Brian was wearing white 'Reebok Classic' trainers, bizarrely coupled with pink/grey socks. Faded blue 'Easy' jeans covered the lower part of his legs; the wide brown belt with silver horseshoe buckle was undone. Down at just below knee level was a pair of black pants, a sort of cross between 'y fronts' and boxer shorts. He was wearing a grey polo shirt with the number '7' embroidered in blue on the left side of the chest. He had a black bin bag tied around his neck in such a way that it could form a back to front 'hoodie', the hood of which had dropped down, away from his face, leaving him wearing an avant garde plastic scarf. The bag also formed the noose which was holding his dead body in an upright position by tying it to a low branch of the tree. The bag was covered in maggots, but also had large amounts of another, pale brown substance, stuck to it. There was an empty tube of 'Evostick' glue with its cap missing, lying on the floor by Brian's left foot.

Brian was a welder by trade, working in the boatyard at Newholme. A single man in his mid-thirties he lived an unremarkable existence. He was a good worker with an excellent attendance record. He largely kept himself to himself, not really socialising with his colleagues apart from the odd after work pint at the 'Seagull and Yardarm' On these occasions he would have a maximum of two pints of lager top, usually with a bag of pork scratchings. He almost invariably left by about half past eight saying

"Sorry lads got to go, I need to get ready for the morning, anyone want a top up before I go". He never said

"Right, I'm off then, see you tomorrow" or even

"Does anyone want a top up 'cause I've got to go? I need to get ready for the morning" but always

"Sorry lads, got to go, I need to get ready for the morning, anyone want a top up before I go"

His mates, such as they were often remarked how Brian was a creature of habit. What none of them knew was exactly what his particular habit was. In their defence however it is unlikely that anyone would have guessed….

Brian had never been very good at attracting the ladies. It had nothing to do with his physique; he was after all a "strapping lad", with the sort of sun bronzed complexion that only comes with regular outdoor work. He had short cropped blonde hair, and eyes the colour of the Mediterranean Sea in the early morning sunlight. Though, it had to be said, the fact that one eye seemed to have a mind of its own and never really look at you, could be a little disconcerting. His problem with the ladies stemmed, it seemed, from his intense shyness, a shyness that showed itself by means of a pronounced st..st…stammer.

This lack of sexual opportunity was easily solved by Brian however; he had built up a large collection of magazines, videos, and latterly, DVDs featuring beautiful ladies who acted out all, well, almost all of his fantasies, and never poked fun of his eye or stutter. I say almost all of his fantasies, there was, for Brian, something very appealing about strangulation and you just could not walk into your local video shop and buy that sort of DVD. Maybe it was a story or letter in one of his magazines that gave him the idea, or maybe it just came to him, in the same way that Sir Isaac Newton got the idea that gravity existed, but either way, Brian discovered that he could get an amazing sexual thrill out of partially strangling himself whilst sniffing glue. The 'buzz' due to a combination of lack of oxygen and high levels of solvent in his blood worked every time. Based on Brian's shopping bills (he was a meticulous hoarder and kept all his receipts stacked neatly in a biscuit tin in his kitchen), he had been indulging in his habit at least three nights a week, until that is, he got it wrong… But at least he died happy, or happier than the poor sod that had to lie between his legs getting a shower of angry maggots drop all over him!

Having recorded the scene as well as I could I wriggled back out of my tree and, in the eerie, not quite darkness, I discussed with Mark Constable, how exactly we were going to recover Brian's body from the tree. I decided that the only option was to cut away the front 'face' of the tree to expose (possibly not the right word in the circumstances) Brian. This would then allow us to cut him down and let his body drop forwards. The first problem was that by now it was too dark to see what we were doing, I thought about the possibility of getting some decent lighting equipment down to us, but soon realised that it would be totally impractical.

"Never mind" I said, "round up all the Maglights you can get your hands on". A 'maglight' is a heavy duty torch carried by policemen on their beats, "and get us some secateurs and a bow saw". Mark made a call on his radio and within about ten minutes a uniformed colleague arrived carrying a Tesco's carrier bag (such is the state of force finances I suppose) in one hand, containing seven of the long black torches and the necessary pruning equipment in the other. I hastily arranged for the torches to be placed in the branches of nearby trees where they shone towards Brian's tree, illuminating the scene like the lights for some strange, open air stage play.

I then did my best Alan Titchmarsh impression and set to work cutting away the branches at the front of the tree to expose Brian's body, carefully moving the cut branches to one side, thus leaving a clear space to lay him once he had been cut down. I considered the problem of bagging the body for transport to the mortuary. There are two accepted methods; the first involves the use of a body bag. This is basically a very large plastic envelope with a zipped flap rather than one that you lick. They normally have three handles on either side for ease of carrying. You unzip the flap, lay your body into the bag and zip it back up again. They are very easy to use in most circumstances, but have the slight drawback of needing a fair degree of precision when placing the body in them. The second method is the 'sausage roll technique'. This involves laying a very large sheet of polythene, approximately ten feet square, on the ground, laying the body on the centre of it, then rolling it up and sealing the ends with tie wraps. The disadvantage of this method is that you have to move the body around more than when using a body bag, with the resultant possibility of moving evidence about. I decided that in the circumstances, the risk of missing a body bag when cutting Brian down far outweighed the risks involved with using a sheet. I was oh so wrong, having failed to take into account some basic rules of physics ... but I digress.

Having laid the sheet on the ground in front of Brian I was faced with the task of cutting him down, this is not as easy as it might seem as I needed to ensure that the knot was preserved. You can gain a lot of information from knots. I also could not simply allow Brian's body to drop to the ground, both for reasons of respect and evidence preservation. Clearly this part of the operation was not going to be a one person task. I called Mark over and after allowing him time to retch a few times, I explained the problem, ending with...

"So, do you want to go behind him and cut him, or hold his shoulders and lower him down". Mark could not decide which task revolted him most, so we decided to solve the dilemma, the way that so many major decisions have been made over the years, we tossed for it, well at least we spoofed for it, which is close enough. For those of you not familiar with spoofing each participant has three coins held behind their back, they produce any number of these coins in a clenched fist and the total number of coins held by all the players is guessed. The winner is the person who guesses correctly; if no one guesses correctly you repeat the process until someone does.

I won. I then made mistake number two, by deciding to send Mark round behind Brian whilst I took his weight. The very second that the noose was cut I realized how silly I had been as the rules of physics I had failed to consider came crashing into my mind... Literally.

when two masses are pushing in opposite directions the greater mass will move the lesser mass

When air cools e.g. At sunset, it holds less water, this water condenses and settles on nearby objects

Friction is reduced when a surface is wet, and plastic doesn't have much friction to start with.

Brian was heavier than me and I was standing on a wet plastic sheet which in turn was lying at a jaunty angle on a steep slope. What happened next seemed to occur in slow motion, as my legs slid from under me and I was propelled over backwards, landing hard on my back with Brian's semi naked body on top of me and embracing me. Our faces met somewhere in the middle of my "Aaaaaaagh" meaning that my mouth was wide open, ready to receive the flow of maggots being shot out of Brian's mouth. It seemed an eternity before I was able to wriggle out from underneath his body, spitting maggots as I went. I looked over to Mark for support but he was unable to help, sitting doubled up on the floor, tears rolling down his face as he laughed hysterically...

An hour or so later, with Brian safely in the coroners ambulance on his way to the mortuary, Mark and I found ourselves off duty and ordering a well-deserved drink.

"What will it be? My round" asked Mark.

"Guinness please". I took one long sip, savouring the creamy white head, and then remembered.....

Ben had not touched a drop of Guinness since; in fact that was when his love affair with good old Scotch had started.

Sunday, March 4th 2007, 8.24 AM

The door to inspector Grieves' office was open but Ben knocked anyway

"Come in Ben, how are things?" Lee asked

"You know" said Ben "Same shit different day. Stitch is being an arse as usual, I've got a headache and some little shit has done a number on half the units on the willow...Oh, and I'm pretty sure we have a murder on our hands."

Grieves frowned "are you sure Ben? The boss isn't gonna like it, what with the recent push to promote the "citizen first" initiative and all that. A murder will really bugger up the divisional crime stats.   You look like shit by the way. Bad night? Don't you think you should go and see Doc Evans, he could get you some counselling?"

"I DONT NEED COUNSELLING ...look, sorry Lee I didn't mean to shout but things are a bit messed up at the moment, and I have a bad feeling about Sandy"

"Sandy?"

"The girl on the beach"

I didn't think we had identified her yet"

"We haven't, look I've got to go, do you want the door shut?"

Sunday, March 4th 2007, 10.13 AM

"Willow Business Park" sounded far nicer than it was. The name conjured up images of converted farm buildings with thatched roofs containing small businesses carrying out such tasks as web site design, picture restoration and clock making. In reality it was a cul-de-sac of three grubby, flat roofed 1960s terraced buildings with rusting metal framed windows. Each building was sub divided into three units, which were in turn rented out to various small businesses.

Unit seven, "Cedar Imports" was similarly named much more grandly than it deserved.

Steve Kampar, the managing director and, much to his chagrin this morning, only key holder for Cedar Imports was a thick set, dark haired man with a hard jaw and a face that matched his mood

"If you lot had done your bloody job properly last time and locked the little sods up when I caught them trying to get in, I wouldn't have had this problem again, ridin' round in your cars is no good, you should be out walkin' around checking decent folks property, bloody useless the lot of you." Ben wished Mr Kampar a good morning and politely asked to see how they had got in this time.

Ben was led to the rear of the building, to a fixed window about two feet square, leading into a store room. This window had no glass in it, nor was there any broken glass on the floor, either inside or outside of it. There was, however, a piece of hardboard which was approximately the same size as the hole in the window, lying on the ground outside. Ben noticed that there was a 'Nike Air Max' shoe mark in mud on this board. Contenting himself with, "Perhaps you should think about getting this window repaired and installing an alarm, especially as this is now the second time they have got in this way." He started his careful examination of the scene.

Cedar Imports lived up to its name in that it did import items, though none of them were made of cedar or any other wood for that matter. The stock held in this warehouse was made mainly of plastic and rubber, imported from China and sold by mail order, or through the type of shops that have blacked out windows and call themselves 'private' or 'gentlemen's shops. Whilst brushing aluminium fingerprint powder over the packaging of a 'realistic' blow up doll called 'Hot Roxanne' Ben let his mind split apart, a trick he had developed over the years. Part of his mind focussed intently on the task in hand, minutely examining the scene for the smallest of clues left behind by the offender; a feint partial fingerprint perhaps, or a hair, a speck of blood, a snagged fibre from his or her shirt. Meanwhile the other part of his mind, working largely subconsciously, looked at the bigger picture, the meaning of these small bits of transferred rubbish left behind at the scene, making mental links between fact and possibility in an attempt to make enough sense of the collected information to enable him to lead his colleagues to the offender.

Today however this part of his mind was wandering, looking at a different picture. This picture was that of a naked female, not 'Hot Roxanne' though the word 'Hot' was probably what triggered the link ... hot ... burn ... Sandy's right hand ... how did you burn your hand Sandy?

Friends sometimes asked Ben if he had nightmares about his work, the honest truth was "No", he had only started having nightmares in the last four months since the car crash that had ended Louisa's, and in a way, Ben's life. Whilst he did not have nightmares about the scenes he witnessed, he was able to recall them on demand with brilliant clarity. He sometimes felt that his mind was like a giant hard drive. All he had to do was to provide the keywords ... hot ... burn and all of the cases filed under those categories popped into his consciousness:

The case of George Upson, who had died of a heart attack then slowly roasted himself in front of the open door of the oven cooking his Christmas Turkey.

The case of Graham Carrow who filled his car with open cans of petrol, poured one can around the car and over himself, and then lit a last cigarette.

The case of Susan Patchett, who made the mistake of smoking in bed, and who's excessive fat acted like the wax in a candle, causing her to be burnt to a skeleton, except for her feet, whilst her bed and the rest of the room remained fairly unburnt, merely covered in a tarry, smoky film and the story of Andrew Henry, the man who led to Ben getting called at 6am, one Sunday morning in late April about ten years ago

Jesus Loves Me

Bringholme North Cliffs were lit by that beautiful light that only occurs just after dawn in the springtime. The Cliff road had been closed at each end by parking a police car diagonally across it. I manoeuvred my van past the car and drove onwards, feeling the small thrill of doing something "naughty" that I always felt when driving down a closed off road, especially when, unfortunately not in this case, I got to drive the wrong way down a dual carriageway. I pulled up straddling the white lines, so as not to disturb any evidence on the verges, about ten feet prior to the start of the skid marks. I got out and spoke to Tom Leadbury, the uniformed collision investigator who had beat me to the scene.

"What have we got Tom? The message from the control room was a bit vague to say the least, something about a car verses pedestrian collision and a fire, is it fatal?"

Tom shook his head "not yet, but according to the paramedics it is only a matter of time, there is no way he's going to make it with those sort of burns"

"So what have we got?"

Tom shrugged "Buggered if I know, that's why I thought I should get you over here. The driver is not making much sense, knocked his head in the accident, why do people never learn about using seatbelts? The other guy is in no fit state to tell us anything."

I was confused, the art of collision investigation, though not a subject that appeals to me, is very precise. It is applied mathematics really, you measure the length of skid marks and areas of damage, on the road and to vehicles involved, draw detailed plans, get your calculator out and using set formulae, work out who hit what where and what speed they were travelling when they collided. Tom was one of the best collision investigators I knew, and in the little over ten years that I had worked with him I had never before heard him resort to "Buggered if I know" when asked to explain how a particular crash had happened.

I got my camera and started to walk towards the green Suzuki 4x4 at the far end of the skid marks, which were about 20 feet long, photographing as I went. When I reached the Suzuki I noticed that its windscreen was cracked *in two places, directly above the steering wheel and next to the pillar on the nearside. There were no bodies, Andrew (though of course, at that stage I did not know his name) and the driver of the Suzuki having been removed to hospital prior to my arrival. A few feet beyond the Suzuki's bonnet was a small area of burnt tarmac. This, then, was the scene of the fire, but what exactly had happened here?*

Looking more closely at the car I noticed that the only damage to it, apart from the broken windscreen was the damage to the radiator grille and nearside of the bonnet. All of this damage was consistent with it having hit a pedestrian who was upright, walking or standing. There was no damage to indicate that any other vehicle had been involved, and then left the scene prior to the arrival of the emergency services. So we have a case of a car hitting a person walking along cliff road, but how then has the person ended up being burnt badly enough to melt the tarmac? Clearly the car had not caught fire and burnt him as there was no burn damage to the vehicle. Had the man been carrying some inflammable liquid which had ignited on impact? Unlikely as there were no signs of an explosion, or of the fire spreading beyond the body. If, for example he was carrying a can of petrol, I would have expected to see burnt remnants of the can and a distinctive "splat" shaped pattern, caused by the petrol running across the tarmac as it burned.

I looked more closely at the broken windscreen. The damage above the steering wheel had been caused from the inside as the drivers head smashed against the glass thinking to himself "If only I'd worn a seatbelt this wouldn't hurt so much"

The other damage was caused from the outside when Andrew was flicked up over the bonnet and head butted the screen. As is often the case, this damage had skin and hair firmly embedded amongst the cracks ... but the hair was burnt. Andrew must have been on fire when he was struck by the Suzuki; perhaps the account from the driver was more sensible than people had given him credit for.

In a collision caused by the driver not paying attention, the point of impact is often just before the start of the skid marks. The bang as the victims face hits the windscreen causes the driver to 'slam on the anchors', the pedestrian is then often carried forward on the bonnet, only to be dumped back onto the road as the car stops. This seemed to be the case here so I walked back up the road with Tom and started to look very closely in the area near to the start of the skid marks. I soon found what I had been looking for, on the verge facing the cliffs I saw a piece of charred skin, part of the sole of one of Andrew's feet that had simply dropped off like a glowing "paper angel" leaving a bonfire.

I set off like some native Indian, tracking game across the prairie. Retracing Andrew's footsteps, which was easy enough to do as the Dewey grass was burned where he had walked. The charred path led in a wide arc towards the cliff edge, passing about eight feet from the edge as it turned back inland, ending up at a small, low walled view point. At various points along the route I found pieces of burnt flesh, hair and clothing. It seemed that Andrews clothes, shoes, and eventually skin, had literally burnt off of him as he walked.

The view point was circular with an opening on the right as you faced the sea. In the middle was the sort of telescope that you put 50 pence in, in order to be allowed to admire the view for a couple of minutes. Around the walls, decorated with 'Shazza woz ere' 'Dons gott a smal willey' and other similar literary works of art was a bench seat where you could sit, clutching your 50p and waiting to be amazed. In amongst the crisp packets and other rubbish in the view point were five bottles of barbecue lighter fluid, a matchbox and a number of fresh spent matches. Looking across to the nearby car park I noticed two cars, one, a red Vauxhall Astra had obviously been abandoned for a week or two, had a smashed rear side window, bare wires hanging below the steering wheel and no radio. Resolving to examine it later in the day I made the radio call that would confirm it to be a stolen vehicle, then I turned my attention to the other car, a deep blue Volvo estate. This car was immaculately cared for both inside and out, neatly parked in the corner bay, with the doors unlocked, keys still in the ignition and a bible on the front passenger seat. Another radio call and I had a fair idea who had been melting the tarmac. The control room operator confirmed my location, identity number and the registration of the Volvo, then after a short pause came back with the fact that the car was not stolen, was insured and MOT'd and belonged to Andrew Henry of 32 Saltwater Way in Bringholme.

Furthermore there was no trace of Mr Henry ever having come to the notice of the police before.

I made a careful fingerprint examination of the bottles of lighter fluid by dusting them with a powder made of minute metal flakes and applied with a magnetic 'wand', recovering the developed fingerprints by covering them with a type of wide sellotape and using it to transfer them to a sheet of clear acetate, a type of plastic. When I had finished examining the bottles in the view point, I walked over to the Volvo and carried out a thorough examination of it as well, looking not only for fingerprints but for any clues as to why Andrew should want to set himself on fire.

My examination of the car involved, amongst other things, flicking through the pages of the bible. Many of the passages were circled with blue pen, one of these was

1CORINTHIANS 16

55 "Where, o death, is your victory?

   Where, o death is your sting?"

Scribbled on a piece of paper stuck into the bible on this page were the words

"I know this to be true.

Death cannot harm me,

I will burn my own cross in the raging sea below

Earth…

Air…

Fire…

and water."

Suddenly it all made sense.

I finished photographing the scene and collecting (more out of decency, than for their forensic value) the pieces of charred flesh and clothing.

Andrew was a manic depressive who had no problems all the time he kept taking his medication. His condition was diagnosed in his early twenties and in the intervening decade and a half he had managed to keep up a good job as purchasing manager for a local coffee wholesaler. He had only had two previous incidents of note, both times ending up with him being sectioned (detained in a secure mental hospital under the provisions of section 136 of the Mental Health Act), once after self-harming by means of using a hammer and nails to create 'stigmata' on his body and the other time after having to be talked away from the edge of the cliffs. Though, that time he was minus the barbecue fluid.

Andrew died in hospital from his burns three days after I made his acquaintance.

It seems that on the morning of his death, Andrew had driven up to the car park at Bringholme North Cliffs, had sat in his car, reading his bible and praying, then taken his bottles of barbeque fluid up to the view point where he had thoroughly doused himself, struck a match, which promptly went out in his shaking hands, then struck another, then another until he finally burst into flame. By now, in considerable pain, he walked towards the cliff edge, ready to throw himself to his death, whilst forcing his body into the shape of a cross. Perhaps the pain disorientated him, or perhaps smoke merely got in his eyes, blinding him, we shall never know. What we do know is that something made him do a wide u turn just before he reached the edge, after which he walked in the opposite direction before falling into the path of an extremely surprised motorist on his way to work.

Ben finished his examination of Cedar Imports, still none the wiser about Sandy's burnt hand. He was good, but some threads were just too thin for even a mind like his to grasp. For the time being this aspect of the case would have to remain a mystery

Sunday, March 4th 2007, 11.21 AM

"Get your arse back here…NOW!" Ben hated his mobile phone most of the time. He especially hated it at the moment, having pulled over to answer it on his journey back from the willow estate. He had almost let it ring but decided to pull over instead. This now seemed to have been a bad decision.

Still shell shocked from the outburst that hit his ear on answering, followed by a click and an ominous silence, Ben knew two things. Firstly that something had seriously pissed Superintendent Smith off, and secondly, that somehow Ben was thought to be to blame. The only thing he didn't know yet, … though he had a feeling that he was going to find out very soon … was exactly what he had done wrong, or more likely, what Stitch had allowed him to be the fall guy for!

Sunday, March 4th 2007, 11.34 AM

Ben pulled up in the rear yard of Bringholme "nick", locked his van because you can never be too careful - there are a lot of dodgy people in police stations, then punched the four digit code into the combination lock of the rear door, took a deep breath and walked to the Superintendent's office. He had considered calling in to see Lee Grieves and asking him what was going on, but decided against it. He was going to find out sooner than he wanted anyway.

The Superintendent's "Come in" that followed Ben's knock, sounded as terse as his earlier tirade over the phone. No sooner had he entered than the 'Boss' was up from his chair, his face looking the colour of tinned tomatoes. He started pacing his office. "Just what the hell is going on Brown? Sergeant Collins from the bureau" (referring to the force fingerprint comparison section) "rang me a few minutes ago and told me he had identified the marks you gave him yesterday from the body on the beach. He has identified them as David Simms. They were supposed to be a bleedin' girl. Now, I've known Jim Collins for a long time, he's a bloody good copper, and wouldn't get something like that wrong, so you must have got the bloody marks mixed up. That's the trouble with you bloody civvies, you just don't have the same standards as policemen. Don't you realise the problems your cock up is going to cause!" Ben was silent for a minute, thinking over what he had just heard and considering what may have happened. All this time the Superintendent's eyes glared at him like a snake preparing to strike.

Then Ben laughed. This was the final straw as far as Superintendent Smith was concerned. "What the hell are you laughing at? This mistake is your last. DO YOU HEAR?"

Ben spoke quietly as he said "Sir, I agree there has been a terrible mistake, I also agree that Sergeant Collins has not made it. He is, as you say, far too good at his job. However, I can assure you that the finger marks he identified were the ones I took from the body on the beach. The man on the beach. Have you heard of gender realignment Sir? I suggest you order a second post mortem because if the first pathologist has got the sex wrong, how will anyone trust the rest of his report. By the way, if you look at the photos you will see that she is not only a he, but is also a murder victim. Hypostasis cannot set in when a body is in the sea. I appreciate you are going to be very busy in the next little while, so I will be in the office writing up the Willow estate jobs if you need me" with that. Ben turned and left the office.

Sunday, March 4th 2007, 6.15 PM

"Today turned into a very good day", thought Ben as he stood at the bar of the 'Fox and Turnip' sipping his Laphroig single malt whisky. "Stitch had managed to make himself look stupid, Ben had managed to put Superintendent Smith in his place and they had a murder to solve to boot. Yes, today had turned into a very good day indeed." Ben wondered how Dr Hopton had managed to make such a drastic mistake. Sex change operations are not that common, but do leave obvious anatomical signs. Dr Hopton was a very experienced Home Office Pathologist and as such should have noticed that something was amiss "down below". It seemed that he had been a victim of the narrow mindedness that is the scourge of anyone doing investigative work. There is a tendency to try and make things fit preconceived ideas. Dr Hopton had assumed that he had a suicide, and as such had assumed he had a female and had not therefore looked as closely as he should have done at the facts before him. Had he kept an open mind whilst carrying out his examination he would have noticed the tell-tale signs of a gender realignment operation and would not have ignored the hypostasis on the body. Keeping an open mind would have caused a murder investigation to be started sooner than it had, and would have allowed Dr Hopton to keep his job.

Don Summers, a regular in the pub and a friend of Ben's sidled over. "I'll buy you a scotch in return for a story" he said.

Cold Case Squad

"It was Christmas eve, the year before last. If you remember it snowed really heavily that year, first white Christmas we had had in ages. By the time I had driven up to the travellers' site at Spring Bottom I was getting worried about driving back, as the snow was coming down really hard, and laying thickly on the road. The wind was beginning to pick up as well, so the snow was being blown around. I swapped my shoes for wellies, pulled on a pair of carefully laundered overalls, and trudged across the site to the remains of the traditional Romany caravan in the far corner, lit by the none too festive glare of halogen lights courtesy of the fire service. Despite the snow and the large amount of water that 'trumpton', who were still in attendance damping down, had sprayed onto the van, it was still smouldering and steaming. On the top of the caravan's access steps, which had strangely remained intact was the charred remains of what at first appeared to be a child, though a closer inspection showed it to be a man, curled into the foetal position and with his lower legs burnt almost completely away by the ferocity of the fire. As the snowflakes hit the body they disappeared with a hiss, but not immediately, thus giving him the appearance of a surreal Dalmatian with moving white spots on a black back. The smell entering my frozen, red nose was like burnt pork sausages forgotten at the end of a barbeque. I checked with the Chief Fire Officer that it was safe for me to erect a scene tent over the remains and to start my examination. I needed to put up the tent in order to preserve any remaining evidence from the worsening weather. Luckily the structure of the van had almost completely been destroyed so it was effectively a flat trailer, low enough for a large scene tent to be erected over the top of it. Unfortunately it was too long so I had no option but to only put up three sides, creating a sort of car port around what was left of the caravan. No sooner had I erected my tent, with the help of two firemen, than the wind decided to drastically increase in strength. Unfortunately the wind was blowing directly into the open end of the tent, turning it from a car port into a parachute, which was then lifted and blown about 100 metres across the site, being chased by myself and a group of cold, wet firemen.

Once the tent was re-erected, and secured with guy ropes and large metal pegs, I started my examination by carefully photographing the scene. Then, with the aid of a small trowel and a much larger fire investigator, I started the painstaking process of carefully sifting through the charred remains of the caravan and its occupant, looking for the smallest of clues as to the cause of the fire and its 'seat', the place where it started. The deepest area of charring was just to the right of where the door to the caravan would have been, close to the small wood burning stove and the position where the body lay. This left me with a small problem, it was equally possible that the victim, burnt beyond recognition, had died trying to escape his burning caravan, or had been murdered on the steps of his caravan before the killer started a fire to destroy the evidence of the crime."

"Hang on a minute" said Don "whatever made you think he had been murdered in the first place?"

"Oh yes, I forgot", answered Ben." Noel Jolly, who's caravan it was and who, it turned out, was the meat in the barbecued caravan, did not have a reputation to match his name. He was far from jolly; in fact he was one of the meanest members of the travelling community ever to set up camp in Spring Bottom. He was believed to be the main supplier of Heroin in the area and was also implicated in handling stolen goods, robbery and firearms offences. Far from being jolly, it was said that the only time he smiled was when he was breaking someone's legs to settle a drugs debt.

We had information that on the day of his death, he had been to Lynton to meet some even more unpleasant people, and that he had not gone there to swap Christmas presents. It seems that one of the people who's legs he had so cheerfully broken, had been employed by these 'Norfolk Boys' as a courier, and they were none to pleased to no longer have a 'mule' with working legs. Noel had returned unscathed, but had been warned that he was not going to have a happy Christmas, and to expect someone other than Santa to come knocking on his caravan door that night. All things considered, murder was a definite possibility.

I think it was as I was carefully digging amongst burnt finger bones, that the pathologist turned up, grumbling about having had his Christmas eve ruined, despite the fact that he was earning considerably more for his visit than anyone else there that night. I was still briefing him as to the circumstances when my mobile phone started ringing. I hate the thing at the best of times, but when crouched over a burnt body in a tent in a blizzard I hate it more than ever. Struggling with frozen fingers to rescue it from my pocket and put it to my ear. I just had time to consider that at least my fingers were still attached to my body, unlike those I had just been collecting up, before it made my day even worse than it already was. I usually like talking to my D.I. Lee Grieves, but today, what he had to say was just about the last thing I wanted to hear. The undercover officers watching the main suspect had reported that his actions meant that if he was to be arrested, it could only be safely carried out in the next few minutes. Grieves needed to know if we had enough evidence to arrest the man.

It was suddenly very important to know if our victim had died as a result of the fire, or if he was dead before it started. There is a very easy way to establish this. You conduct a post mortem examination, during which you cut open the trachea … windpipe … and look for soot. If you find it, you know the person was alive and breathing smoke during the fire, if you don't find soot, the person must have been dead before the fire started. The problem we faced however was that we simply did not have time to move the body to the mortuary to carry out the post mortem examination. So, after a brief discussion, I found myself holding a Maglight torch as steady as my shivering hands would allow, whilst the pathologist cut open the dead man's throat. All the time we were doing this the wind was driving snow through the open side of our flimsy shelter. Once the cut had been made and the inside of the windpipe examined, our roles were reversed. The pathologist became the lighting engineer and I took the role of camera man trying to record the black sooty marks inside, before ringing D.I. Grieves to tell him that I was as happy as I could be that, untimely as the death was, it was unlikely to be a murder. I still could not confirm that the victim was Noel Jolly; it wasn't until after the holiday period was over that a full post mortem examination was carried out, and dental impressions taken to prove the identity of the body. This post mortem showed very high alcohol levels in Noel's body, almost fatal levels by themselves. The most likely explanation is that, extremely drunk, he decided to stoke up his fire, accidentally igniting newspapers known to be stored near to it. In a confused drunken panic he tried to find his way out of his van, past the worst of the fire, finally becoming overcome by the smoke and dying inches from safety. Now I think I'll have that scotch" said Ben "Best make it a double"

Monday, March 5th 2007, 09.00 AM

Once again Ben found himself in the Mortuary at Bringholme General Hospital. He had woken up with a hangover and had not had any breakfast. He knew this was a mistake as today was going to be the second post mortem examination carried out on Sandy, or David, as he had now been identified. After 5 days in a mortuary fridge and god knows how long in the sea beforehand, David was not going to look or smell very nice at all. Ben raided the fridge in the mortuary office and took a Mars Bar and can of Red Bull. He would replace them later, but now his need was greater than their rightful owners. After a briefing with Dr Field, one of the large fridges in the ante room to the mortuary was opened and David's body, in its white plastic body bag, looking like the chrysalis of some exotic giant butterfly, was slid out on a stainless steel stretcher, placed on a trolley and brought round to the mortuary table for examination. Ben wondered why they were called tables when in fact they bore more resemblance to a long, thin, shallow sink made of porcelain, and with a plug hole at the foot end.

As the zip of the body bag was opened, so that Ben and the mortuary assistant could lift the body across onto the table, he wished he had not drunk so much the night before. The smell was sickly and cloying, David looked to be covered in green bruises, the result of his starting to decompose. His face looked much like it had in the photographs taken on the beach, but there was a 'y' shaped line of very coarse stitches running from his ears, down the centre of his chest and stomach to her vagina. Sam, the mortuary assistant, cut the top stitch below each ear and then unpicked the line of stitches as easily as if she were preparing to turn up the hem on a pair of trousers. As she reached into the chest cavity to remove the yellow bin bag containing David's assorted organs, the smell got much worse. Ben took a step backwards and tried hard to only take small breaths for a minute. "Thank god this is a second post mortem", thought Ben "at least the stomach has already been emptied".

Ben could cope with most sights and smells, but he could not, even after all these years, see vomit or a persons decanted stomach contents without gagging. Today, with his hangover, would not be a good day to test to see if he had developed a stronger stomach than previously.

Monday, March 5th 2007, 10.07 AM

"Well that just about sews it up" said Dr Field. Then, looking across at Sam "Thanks, Sam, you can sew her, er, him up now. Gentlemen, shall we resume to the office for a chat?"

The post mortem examination had taken a little over an hour, and had been very revealing. Dr Field had confirmed that Sandy had indeed been born a man and had undergone a sex change operation, getting Ben to take a close up photograph of the body's pubic region, to show the presence of an inverted urethra to prove his point. He had also noticed a fracture to the back of David's skull, and that the burn to his right fingers was more severe than the burn on his palm, with the burn to the palm having a curious straight edge to it. He also felt that, due to changes to the skin tissue of the hand, the burn was caused after death, but said he would need to carry out further microscopic examinations before he could say for certain.

Ben was concerned by the fractured skull. Yes, there was now a sensible cause of death, but it left many unanswered questions, especially in the light of the burnt hand most probably having occurred after death. How were the two connected? The burn did not appear to be the result of deliberate mutilation, and there was just the one fracture, again it did not have the hallmarks of a determined attack on David. How had he met her untimely end? Ben was reminded of another case involving a fractured skull, but that case was easier, he had had a scene to examine and more importantly, a story to examine. In this case he had neither to help him, just a body with a cracked skull and singed fingers. The other case had started off quite simply with someone admitting to a crime.

I Think I Might Have Hurt My Girlfriend

"I think I may have hurt my girlfriend. I came home yesterday dinnertime and she was sitting in the chair doing a crossword and no sign of me dinner anywhere and well I just flew" said the man standing at the counter of Bringholme police station, his voice shaky with obvious fear, and a desire to get his story told as quickly as possible. *"You would, wouldn't you and there was this lump hammer. We, well I, had been doing some work in the kitchen just lately and had been using it to chisel out the wall for some new wiring and she gave me some lip and I just couldn't help it. I hit out and well the hammer was in my hand and well I think it hit her, once or maybe twice and then I panicked and left and, well I've been ringing and there's no reply and, well I was wondering if you would go round and check she's ok."*

A PC had been sent round, and as a result an ambulance had been called, and once they had confirmed that the lady in question was dead, I had been dispatched to the scene. When I had parked my van and changed into a paper suit, mask, gloves and overshoes, I walked over to the back door where PC Tomkins was on guard. Newly promoted Detective Inspector Lee Grieves, who had recently transferred from Coomstoft, strode across with his chest puffed out. This was the first major case that he had been put in charge of.

"Ah SOCO, glad you are here, look, we shall pop in and have a look around, then I will leave you to do whatever you have to do. Come on"

"Right sir, I will go and get you a suit"

"I am not going to wear one of those bloody things."

"That's fine Sir, but you might want to call up for some new clothes and shoes, because if you step foot into my scene without suiting up, I will be putting your clothes into bags the moment you come out. Or of course, you could wait out here for a couple of minutes, and take the video back with you to watch at the nick with a cup of tea."

Lee Grieves waited for the video and from that day on never asked to come into a scene again. We became firm friends from that moment on.

As I walked carefully around the scene, recording it's every detail on my video camera; it became clear that the man at the police station had not been exactly telling the truth.

The first time you hit someone with a hammer, rather disappointingly, no blood is transferred to the weapon; it takes a second or two for the blood to leak out of the wound. However, the second time you hit the victim, the hammer gets covered in blood, and this blood flicks off when you pull the hammer back for the third strike. When this flicked off blood hits a wall or ceiling it leaves a distinctive mark, looking like an exclamation mark, with the dot pointing in the direction that the blood was travelling. The thickness of the mark in relation to its length shows the angle at which the blood hit the surface, meaning that you can accurately calculate where the blood started its travel.

My video effectively showed the scene in reverse. The first thing it showed was the rear hall containing the body of the victim, Linda Carter, lying in the hallway in a pool of blood with her face barely recognisable under the mass of bloody matted hair. Passing through the kitchen, it then showed the lounge and the chair that Linda had been sitting in prior to the attack. This chair had drops of blood on it, along with Linda's broken and blood spattered glasses. Next to the chair was an opened puzzle magazine, again blood stained with a 'Save the Children' pen lying beside it. The wall behind the chair, and the ceiling above it, bore the exclamation mark shaped 'directional cast off' marks that would be expected given his story. However, the wall and ceiling on the other side of the room, next to the kitchen door also had cast off marks. The wall also had bloody finger marks close to the doors opening edge, near to the position of the latch.

The kitchen ceiling was clean of blood, but the walls had cast off marks on them, though the highest was seven feet above the floor. Again there were bloody finger marks near to the door to the hall. Linda was lying on her front in the hall, with her head towards the back door, her feet still just inside the kitchen and her face turned to her left. Both hands were forward of her head, and it appeared that she may have tried to pull herself towards the back door. The blood staining in the hall was, as you would expect, much heavier, the deep crimson colour contrasting uncomfortably with the lilac painted walls, and in this enclosed space the coppery smell of spilt blood laid heavily in the air. The staining on the walls was again mainly in the form of cast off marks, and was concentrated near to Linda's head. None of this staining extended more than three feet above the floor. There were bloody shoe marks on the floor between Linda's head and the rear door, pointing out of the scene.

Blood patterns are very good at explaining the sequence of events when people have been assaulted, and these stains were crying out to tell me the last few moments of Linda's life. I listened with my eyes and imagination, and the grim tale went like this.

Linda had, as her boyfriend Paul had said, been sitting in the chair in the corner of the lounge doing a crossword when he entered. She may have stood up to greet him, only he knows for sure, but his first blow with the hammer knocked her back into the chair. It was most likely this blow that knocked her glasses from her face, and caused her magazine to fall to the floor. At this point she would have put her hands up to her head, in a vain attempt to defend herself. Her fingers being covered in the blood from her wound, before being crushed by the second blow from the hammer. Linda got up again, trying to run from her attacker, and made it as far as the kitchen door, presumably slammed shut by Paul as he entered the room. As she fumbled with her crushed and bleeding fingers to lift the latch, her vision blurred both by the pain from the hammer blows, and the blood running into her eyes, Paul caught up with her and hit her again, at least three times, judging by the bloodstains. Somehow she managed to open the door and stagger; half crouched over, across the kitchen. As she tried to escape, Paul continued to rain blows onto her head, with his heavy lump of cast iron on a stick. As she reached the hall she fell forward, perhaps fainting from the pain, or perhaps being callously pushed over by her assailant. Paul then stood over her body and repeatedly swung his hammer. Her skull cracking open, like a chocolate egg in the hands of a three year old on Easter Sunday morning.

The post mortem examination had showed that Paul had hit Linda at least eighteen times, though that was a conservative estimate, given the damage to her skull and the fact that some wounds may have been hidden by later ones.

Despite his easily disproved attempt to claim it had been a short lived crime of passion, I don't think Paul was lying about everything. I do agree that, yes, he may have hurt his girlfriend... Just a bit.

Monday, March 5th 2007, 10.42 AM

Ben drove back from the mortuary deep in thought. The screech of brakes and blast of the horn as he jumped a red light without realising it brought him back to his senses.

Jumping red lights is never a good idea, especially when a petrol tanker is crossing your path, and even more especially when you are driving a marked police van. The near miss caused Ben to pull over, covering his eyes with his hands, imagining the chaos that would have occurred if the tanker had arrived half a second earlier.

Ben sat parked on the side of the Bringholme bypass until his heart slowed, and his legs stopped shaking. Looking carefully in his mirror, he pulled out into the heavy flow of traffic and headed back to the station.

Ben thought no more of David during that day, it was a typical Monday, and lots of commercial premises had been broken into over the weekend, and needed examining as soon as possible. The late start due to the post mortem had not helped matters. Nor had Stitch who, being first in, had taken the opportunity to claim all of the decent jobs, the scenes where there was a good possibility of obtaining forensic evidence, whilst leaving Ben the jobs which were unlikely to yield much, apart from a complaint about late attendance. Ben had spent the day trying to appease victims of crime, who felt that he should have got there quicker and found more evidence (despite their tidying up of the crime scene). He had politely responded to such comments as "You lot should spend more time catching burglars, than wasting taxpayers money hounding me just cause I was doing just over 30 in a 30 limit" and "Glad you could finally be bothered to turn up, but you might as well sod off, some of us have a living to earn, and I have had to tidy everything up while you have been popping round to one of your tea stops". All the time Ben had wanted to reply with "I've spent most of the morning up to my elbows in the insides of a rotting corpse, so don't tell me about your bad day pal" but had kept this urge under control in the interests of keeping his job.

Monday, March 5th 2007, 6.34 PM

Ben finally got back to the office, only slightly consoled about his long and tiring day, by the fact that he didn't have a wife or girlfriend to nag him about his late arrival home. He walked into the office, straight through to the examination room, and flicked the kettle on. Whilst it was boiling he picked up the phone to listen to any messages that had been left. There were three, the first was a PC, asking if a result had come back from the forensic laboratory, for the shoes that Stitch had sent off, in relation to a case where a man had been severely kicked outside Bringholme's only nightclub, the Strandline. Ben ignored that; Stitch could sort it in the morning. The second was a very high pitched ladies voice saying "Hello, is that the CSI squad, I was told you would come and look at my car this morning, it is now..." Ben deleted that message; he had already had the pleasure of this particular ladies view on his late arrival earlier, in person, and had no desire to hear her moan over the phone as well. The third was one that he could not ignore "Brown. Superintendent Smith here, I need to speak to you as soon as you get this message. Don't you ever answer your bloody radio or mobile phone?"

Ben climbed the stairs to the first floor, two at a time as quickly as he could, not because he was in a hurry to hear whatever Superintendent Smith thought was so important for him to hear, but because he always climbed the stairs like that. He felt that it was his daily exercise, enabling him to convince his conscience that it was OK to drink as heavily as he did. "As long as you keep fit and do regular exercise, the odd drop of scotch isn't going to hurt you". He knew he was lying to himself, but didn't really care. Since the night that Louisa had had the accident, no .... "For once in your life be honest" he told himself ... since the night that Louisa ... that she ... killed herself ... that he had allowed her to kill herself ....

The tears nearly came then, but remembering where he was, and who he was going to see, he quickly managed to pull himself together. He had learnt over the years to shut down all emotion instantly when it was necessary. You could not do this job for long without being able to shut off. However, this ability, this trick of turning to stone came with a heavy price tag. He knew exactly what the cost was, but now was not the time to dwell on it. That time would come later, in the early hours of the morning, when he couldn't sleep yet again, and would end up sitting in his 'thinking chair' discussing it with his old friend Mr Whisky.

Ben decided, as his knock was answered, that Superintendent Smith had 'abrupt' as his only conversational style. He imagined Smith on his wedding night, his bride, lying in bed expectantly saying "Graham darling, I've waited so long for tonight, are you coming to bed with me?"

"Yes but make it quick"

Trying not to laugh, twice in as many days might be pushing his luck a bit; Ben entered the Superintendent's office.

"Brown, there has been a development, we found a boyfriend, seems they split up recently, very messy separation apparently. We are lifting him tomorrow morning (referring to the fact that they had a warrant for the boyfriends arrest), I have arranged for Stitch to SOCO his house, as you have been with the victim today and we don't want any contamination of the evidence do we, there have been enough cock ups already. Well, unless you have any questions I have a lot to do, good day"

Superintendent Smith turned to his computer and started typing; leaving Ben in no doubt that any questions would not be welcomed, so he contented himself with "Thanks for letting me know" and left the room, hoping that his muttered "arsehole" was covered by the door shutting behind him as he left.

Ben was furious. Yes, fair enough, Stitch had started this case but it was his ineptitude that had meant Ben had needed to get involved. It had been Ben who had showed that it was a case of murder, and not the result of a sex game gone wrong, as stupidly proposed by Stitch. Now Stitch was going to get the glory of an arrest scene, whilst Ben most likely would have to spend the day examining cars, where the owners had been too daft to realise that using keys to lock doors helps avoid having your sat nav nicked.

Stitch, the mighty CSI who could not even tell the difference between a suicide, sex game gone wrong and murder. Stitch, who did not realise that hypostasis does not form in bodies floating in the sea, stitch, who would never let go of the fact that he was in on the arrest, Stitch who ..... "No. Enough" Ben told himself, with so much force that it nearly came out loud "granted, Stitch is a devious little shit, who is not very good at his job, but in fairness this is a very complicated case. Stitch is young, ambitious and inexperienced, and the job is all about experience" Ben remembered a case that had taxed his abilities earlier in his career, when he was also young, ambitious and inexperienced. Ben had, in that case, done the opposite to what Stitch had done in this, Stitch had talked a murder down to an accident, and Ben had talked an accident up to a murder. He wondered what was in fact worse.

The call had been to a road traffic collision, where the victim had been burnt to death.

Crashing Out

"Hi Ben, it's the control room here, sorry for waking you up but we need you to come out to a fatal (referring to a car crash where someone had died)" It was 5 in the morning and I had slept badly, partly because it was so warm and muggy, and partly because I had spent the first part of the night with Louisa. I had been seeing her for about a month now, and had nearly managed to convince her to stay the night. She had finally left about two hours earlier despite my asking her, no, begging her to stay.

I grumpily took the necessary details and wearily got dressed, waking up as I drove to the police station to collect my van, then on to the scene, which was where the main road between Bringholme and Lynton passes through limekiln wood. The car was burnt out, both of the offside doors were open which seemed a little strange, but may of course been due to the actions of the fire service. I started to examine the scene more closely, taking in the finer details. The car was a blue Citroen Saxo. It had come to rest with its bonnet in a tree; there was however, only slight damage to the front end, so the impact had not been very hard. Looking back at the road, there was a slight right hand bend. The road was uniformly grey, there were absolutely no skid marks, it seemed as though the car had simply gently driven off of the road into the tree, with no attempt to steer away or slow down... suicide?

Turning my attention back to the Citroen, I asked the fire crew about the doors. I was told that the doors were open when they arrived; all they had had to do was damp down the well-established fire. I looked into the car, the driver's seat, or what remained of it, was empty. There was no sign of the seat belt having been fastened. The ignition key, whilst badly melted by the heat was in the off position. The thing that gave most cause for concern was the rear seat. Lying across it was the charred remains of a person. I took the body to be male, but it was charred beyond any further recognition. In the debris of the boot space, was the melted remains of a plastic 5 litre petrol can, although it now consisted of a grotesquely twisted black cap, sitting atop a green blob of molten plastic.

"Let's get this straight" I said to the traffic inspector "We have a slow speed collision with a tree, involving a car with its engine turned off, and no driver, that has caused the car to burst into flames killing its passenger, a passenger,

who could easily have escaped through an open door….I do not like this at all, I think our man was murdered"

Even as I was taking the necessary photographs, calls were being made to the on call Detective Inspector, who in turn was calling Superintendent Smith and arranging staffing for a major incident room.

There was nothing in the form of shoe marks around the car, apart from some obvious fireman's boot marks. The burnt state of the little Saxo meant that there was practically no chance of recovering fingerprints or DNA, or for that matter any other evidence. I thought that once the body had been moved there may be a slim chance of recovering something from the area where he had lain, as his body would have acted as a bit of a heat shield, though even this was unlikely, as he was on a sprung seat, so it would probably have burnt from the bottom up as well. The post mortem examination would hopefully tell us exactly how he had been killed, which in turn might give us something to go on. I asked for a police dog to be called to the scene, to try and find some form of track from the vehicle and hopefully, some discarded weapon. I also arranged for a coroners ambulance to be put on standby, to transport the body to the mortuary once I had bagged him up.

It was about 40 minutes later by the time that Kane had finished his search of the scene, along with PC Grimshaw, his handler. I had left Kane alone to do his part of the job. I was never really happy with the way he looked at me as though I was his   next meal. I used the free time to grab a desperately needed strong coffee, using the kettle in the back of the collision investigation transit van that had been brought to the scene by the traffic officers. I was in dire need of a sausage and egg roll as well, but the 'traffic canteen' didn't run to such luxuries, so I told my rumbling stomach that I could always get one from the 'Lighthouse Lantern Café' on the high street, on my way to the mortuary in an hour or so.

Then with the aid of a rather unwilling PC, I removed the victim from the back seat of the Saxo and placed him in a body bag, which I had laid next to the rear offside door. PC Dealer and I then carried the bag to the coroner's ambulance, waiting on the tarmac. Burnt bodies are surprisingly light, so the weakness induced by my lack of sleep and lack of food was not a problem, the smell of cooked meat, however did make my stomach rumble even more loudly than before.

"Right lads, who is going to be coroner's officer then?" I asked

The traffic inspector looked directly at PC Dealer, who, it appeared, was having a much worse day than me, and said "Stuart, I think it would be good for you to take this one on" then turning to me "Why do you ask?"

At this point I told a little white lie "We will need continuity of the body, someone is going to have to follow the ambulance to the mortuary and book him in. Normally I would be happy to do it, but I've got to nip back to the nick and get a post mortem kit. So I can't, Stuart" turning to him with a straight face "Sorry, mate you will have to do it. Speak to Sam and she will make you a cuppa if you ask her nicely. I will be about half an hour at the most"

It was nearer to 45 minutes later when I pulled into the car park behind the mortuary. Before I got the post mortem kit out from the box, immediately behind the driver's seat where it was always kept, I carefully checked in the rear view mirror, to make sure there were no tell-tale signs of dripped egg yolk or brown sauce on my chin.

Two hours later, when the post mortem was finished, I was beginning to look at a whole new picture in relation to this case. A picture which, though bizarre, was a lot less sinister than I had initially imagined. Our man had been aged in his sixties or seventies and had died of a heart attack; there was a little smoke in his lungs, indicating that he may have been alive during the early part of the fire. There was evidence that he has been a heavy smoker during his life. There were no traumatic injuries to his body. Apart of course from the severe burns.

"Bugger", I thought, "I am going to look seriously stupid here; the old fool hasn't been murdered after all"

Whilst the post mortem was being conducted, the enquiry into the man's death was moving on apace. A vehicle examiner from the traffic police department had looked at the Saxo, having recovered it to the workshops at the police station, and had managed to find an engine number. A check on the Driver and Vehicle Licensing Authority computer in Swansea had provided an index mark for the vehicle, more commonly known as a registration number, and this number had yielded an owner. Frederick Cartwright from an address in Carnborough, about 20 miles from Bringholme. Officers had been dispatched to his address where they were met by his widow. (Though she did not know this yet) The appearance of two detective constables on her doorstep at breakfast time, gave her a bit of a clue that all was not well. Elsie Cartwright confirmed that her husband was the owner of the blue Saxo. Her "My Fred is all right isn't he, he's not in any trouble?" was met with "I'm afraid there has been a bit of an accident, we think your husband might be involved. Look, is there anyone I can ring? A son or daughter perhaps? Sit down, let me make you a cup of tea and I will tell you all about it"

The conversation that followed resulted in two things, an ambulance being called for Elsie Cartwright who was in deep shock and having difficulty breathing, and the detectives learning that her beloved Fred would sometimes, when he was having trouble sleeping, get up at around half past three and drive into Bringholme to the fish docks to watch the morning catch being unloaded and to try and get a bargain at the fish market. Elsie always worried when he did this as he wasn't as fit as he used to be, having poor eyesight and a dodgy heart. He had already had two scares earlier that year and she was worried what would happen if he broke down and had to walk any distance. She told the officers that her protests had always been met with "Don't worry love, it's not far and I always carry a can of petrol in the back, along with my coat and stick."

An assistant divisional officer from the Lynton and Bringholme Fire and Rescue Service had also examined the recovered car. He concluded from the pattern of burning that the fire has most probably been the result of a flammable vapour explosion, which in turn had blown open the nearside doors and smashed all of the windows. Things pointing to this included the fact that the glass fragments had sharply broken edges, rather than melted ones and the door latches were bent and damaged.

The strange and unfortunate series of events leading to Fred Cartwright's death almost certainly went something like this. Having spent a sleepless night due to the muggy weather Fred had decided to go on one of his early *morning fishing, or at least fish buying, expeditions. He had kissed his beloved Elsie goodbye for the final time. An act which, sadly, she slept through. He then got dressed, went downstairs, made himself a cup of tea, scalding the pot first and then leaving it to brew for just the right amount of time before pouring it, then adding a flat spoonful of sugar, before finally adding a dash of full fat milk.*

Fred was a naturally particular person in everything he did, and could not bear to drink tea that had been made in anything other than the "proper" way.

He then got his coat and walking stick from the hallway, removed his wallet from the sideboard drawer and placed it in his coat pocket, and went out to his car.

After carefully checking all was in order, including a quick check that he had enough spare fuel in the boot "just in case"... he started to drive to Bringholme, most probably listening to the BBC world service on the car radio.

As he was driving through Limekiln woods he felt a pain, more of tightness really, in his chest. Involuntarily, due to the pain he clutched at his chest, taking his hands off the wheel only for a second, but long enough for the car to leave the road on the outside edge of the curve. Fred grabbed the wheel again and applied the brakes. The crash into the tree was very gentle but shook, and the pain in his chest caused Fred to sit, dazed for a couple of minutes. When he came to his senses he thought he could vaguely smell petrol but it didn't register that the smell was coming from the can in the boot space that had fallen over when the car hit the tree and had started to leak from the cap that had not been properly tightened by Fred after he had checked it prior to his journey.

Deciding that he would have to walk to find help Fred unbuckled his seatbelt and turned off the ignition "You can never be too careful" he thought to himself. He then got out, rather unsteadily due to his shortness of breath, and went to the back offside door. Feeling none too well, he decided that a cigarette may just calm his nerves. He took the packet from his jacket pocket before realising that he had left his matches in his coat pocket. He opened the door, only to find that the impact had knocked his coat and walking stick off of the seat into the foot well on the nearside. He clambered in, and retrieved his coat whereupon another wave of nausea crept over him. "I really don't feel too good" he thought "time to light this fag"

As he struck the match his last ever thought was "I really should give up, these things will be the death of me"

Ben didn't bother to make the cup of coffee that he had boiled the kettle for. Instead, deciding that he would bend a few rules and sort out the paperwork and exhibits from today's jobs in the morning he turned off the lights in his office, locked the door and headed to the 'Fox and Turnip' for a meeting with his old friend Glen Morangie.

Tuesday, March 6th 2007, 6.58AM

At this precise moment in time, Ben hated one thing in life more than he hated Stitch and that one thing was his alarm clock. As every nerve in his head was tortured by a pounding base line he resolved to write to the managing director of 'The Coast FM' and ask what kind of deranged programme planner would decide to play 'Bat Out of Hell' at that time of the morning. Ben thumped the snooze button and rolled himself back into his duvet.

"I feel like shit" Ben said to himself.

He started to feel sorry for himself at this point, as so often happened when he woke up with a stinking hangover. "Now Louisa has gone there really is no one to worry about me" Ben had not spoken to his parents, well, to his mother at least, in over ten years, since the incident at his father's funeral. Drink had played a part in that as well. Ben's heart cried out to him to just ring her up and say sorry before it was too late, but his head was too stubborn to listen.

"As far as the world is concerned, nobody would care if I just laid here and died in bed" thought Ben " It is not as if I even have a dog to pine for me when I am gone, my life has become totally worthless to anybody" He decided that if the flat wasn't so damn cold he might just go to the bathroom cabinet and empty the pot of paracetamol tablets down his throat, but as the bed was warm and cosy he would settle for just a few more minutes wrapped up warm instead. As Ben lay there listening to the thumping of his pulse in his temples he wondered what stupid theory the mighty Stitch would come up with if Ben were found dead in bed. Ben was fully aware that sometimes the explanation of a case is much more mundane than the circumstances

lead you to believe.

It's Easy When You Know The Answer

I looked around the room. It was the master bedroom of a tastefully converted barn. The early morning sunlight streamed in through the large picture window on the Eastern wall. The view through this window could only be described as spectacular, with the golden disc rising behind the tree lined hills marking out their wooded summits in stark silhouette. Inside, the scene was equally peaceful, there was no sign of disturbance anywhere, save for the door which had been forced to gain entry. I noted that the lock was a mortise lock with the key, a large, old, ornate one still in place on the inside of the door. As such it would have been virtually impossible to lock from the outside when exiting. I say the scene was peaceful and indeed a first glance showed it to be so, but a closer inspection told a different story. The lady lying on the bed was on her back dressed in a nightgown. The gown was undisturbed so it seemed unlikely that she had been the victim of a sexual assault, this idea was supported by the fact that she had been sleeping with her three pet rottweillers in the bedroom with her. It would be a very brave sexual killer to commit a crime in such circumstances. However, there was no doubting that she had been suffocated, the wide staring eyes with bright red pin pricks of blood, staining the whites (a phenomena known as petechiae) gave a clear indication of this as a cause of death. She had also pulled desperately at the sheets, which were rucked up around the body, and presumably at her attacker in an attempt to get free as the last breath was squeezed from her body.

When you are suffocated you become unconscious after about twenty seconds, this may not seem very long, but try this, breathe out as hard as you can, hold your breath and count out in your head "one desperate struggle...two desperate struggles..," keep going till you reach twenty. To make it more realistic try exercising at the same time, then try to imagine the panic you would feel knowing that no matter how much your lungs burned and your brain screamed for desperately needed air, you were not going to get any.

Looking at Vanessa Powell I looked at the desperately pulled sheets and imagined that panic and the scene both inside and outside the room took on a much more sinister air.

There is a well-known brain teaser involving a dead man in a locked room, lying in a pool of water. I was reminded of that as I examined this scene. How was it possible for someone to have entered, attacked and killed Vanessa in the presence of her guard dogs, then leave unscathed, locking the door from the inside? The window perhaps? Double glazed, closed and locked from the inside. The room was on the first floor, so access would have had to be made using a ladder. An earlier look around the outside had shown there to be no marks in the flower bed, of the sort I would have expected if a ladder had been used to gain entry. Sherlock Holmes was quoted as saying that once you have eliminated all other possibilities, the only one left, no matter how implausible must be the answer. I was therefore satisfied that the killer was safely in custody already, having been removed from the scene by a neighbour of Ms Powell. A neighbour much braver than me. This was confirmed when I looked at Vanessa's clenched right hand and saw a small clump of short black hair. Vanessa had been killed by one of her dogs, not murdered, but killed by an attempt at kindness.

Vanessa was single and in her late fifties when she died. She had been married but the marriage had ended, fairly amicably, a few years earlier. Since that time she had lived a comfortable yet quiet existence with her dogs as her only companions. She worked from home translating texts. She rarely went out other than to walk her dogs across the nearby hills or to buy clothes. She bought her food on line and had it delivered weekly to her door. She had few visitors due, in part, to the presence of the dogs, which despite their appearance and the reputation of the breed were actually quite friendly. The main reason for her solitude was that she preferred her own company and had a rather abrupt manner when dealing with others.

Vanessa seemed to be a healthy lady to those who watched her take the dogs for their regular long walks. She had a slim frame and sprightly step, but unknown to all but her doctor and a few close friends, she had a weak heart. On the night of her death she had gone to bed as usual at about 1 am. She was a very light sleeper. Her dogs slept on the bed with her. Perhaps she was not feeling well and the dogs sensed it, no one will ever know for sure, but one of the dogs evidently decided to comfort his mistress by lying close to her. By lying, in fact across her chest.

Now your average male rottie weighs in at about 50 kilogrammes, or eight stone, approximately the same weight as Vanessa herself. There was no way that she, with her weak heart, could push her pet off of her and as such she was slowly smothered by her devoted pet who was only trying to keep his mistress warm... One desperate breath ... two desperate breaths ...

Ben wondered if the answer to David's death was as mundane, he would find out later that same day.

Tuesday, March 6th 2007, 4.32 PM

Ben was sitting in the office, morosely writing up the endless paperwork generated by his attendance at the day's rash of burglaries and stolen cars when Stitch entered.

"The results of the second interview just came in, it's just like I said" gloated stitch "seems David and his boyfriend, Adrian, I mean, who shags someone called Adrian, and he's ginger, split up about a month ago. On the day of the murder David shows up at Adrian's to collect some CD's and shit, they have a row and Adrian clouts him, knocks him back against the kitchen door frame and knocks him out. Panics and fucks off out, coming back about ten hours later to find his ex, still on his back, dead on the kitchen floor with his right hand pressed against the fire box door of their Rayburn, Adrian thinks … oh bugger… strips him off, goes and gets the weights from the gym they had set up in the garage, along with a length of chain" a pause, followed by a grin "god knows what they had used that for previously, anyway, he bungs him in the boot of his car and slings him off of the cliffs above Devils steps. He's in cell two at the moment sobbing his heart out having coughed the lot… Another case under the belt of Stitch and Co. We're going for a celebration beer later if you want to come along. Stick with us professionals and you might learn something"

Ben got up, walked up to Stitch, invading his personal space "Couldn't hope to compete mate … must have been a really odd sex game, you arrogant tosser … go have a drink with your mate Smith, I'm off."

With that Ben turned and walked out of the office not having the pleasure of seeing the open mouthed expression of shock on the face of Mark Stitch.

Epilogue

Thursday 13th September 2007 4.07PM

"It's been a funny old day" said Ben as he shut the door to the office "what was that TV programme with the shopkeeper who said that at the end of each episode?"

"Open All Hours" offered Colin Upsern "Fancy a pint?"

Ben was really tempted. He really liked Colin, who had come down from the DNA unit at headquarters to replace Stitch after his transfer to Avon and Somerset police force. Colin had a lot to learn about the job, there was no question about that, but he was keen and intelligent and had 'a good eye for a scene'. The main thing that Ben liked about him however was his honesty. With Colin, what you saw was what you got. There was no hidden agenda, no duplicity and no bullshit.

"Sorry mate, you know I can't think of anything better than watching you get ratted and make a fool of yourself in front of Gloria" (referring to the barmaid down the Fox and Turnip, who Colin fancied like mad) "But I have already got a date. How about tomorrow though?"

"Anyone we know?"

"No, but she is really special, way out of your league. See you in the morning"

Thursday 13th September 2007 6.27PM

The rain was falling steadily as Ben arrived for his meeting. He made a strange sight as he sat cross legged on the grass with the rain mixing with his tears.

"Louisa, we have got to talk. I should have said this a long time ago. If I had, we would not be here now. I really don't know how to start, you know what I am like, I get all muddled and tongue tied, I'm drinking less nowadays by the way, I eased off after the body on the beach job, and, well......" his voice trailed off, for a couple of minutes the silence was broken only by the sound of the rain and Ben's quiet sobs then he took a deep breath to compose himself.

"I love you; I have loved you every minute since we met. I will always love you and one day we will meet up again; do they have SOCOs in heaven? I am really sorry, I should have noticed how you felt but I was too wrapped up in me. I can't turn the clock back, you know I would if I could, but I can't, but neither can I continue punishing myself. You were ill and I should have helped you, I didn't and I am sorry but it's done, I can't bring you back but I can bring me back" another pause punctuated by sobs "Goodbye Louisa"

Ben gently kissed the headstone, stood up and walked off "I think the Lighthouse Lantern will still be open. I think I might just pop in and grab a coffee.

Thursday 13th September 2007 7.42PM

Ben sat in his thinking chair. On the table next to him was a large glass of diet Coke. His laptop was open on his lap and he was gently typing away. Long thoughtful pauses punctuated the tapping. After half an hour he stopped and read the passage in front of him, changing the spelling and grammatical mistakes highlighted by little red and green squiggles on his screen. He also re worded a couple of sentences that he had decided did not sound quite right.

Something was wrong; he just couldn't put his finger on it. John Swimmer looked at the images again. The cover of the photograph album read:

"Unknown female   01.03.07   Bringholme bay CSI Carne"

Technically they were perfect; Mark Carne was a good photographer, a complete arse, but a good photographer. Even so, something was very wrong with the photographs; John just couldn't work out what. On the face of it the scene photographs showed a simple suicide; a naked female washed up on the beach, not badly decomposed, with few obvious injuries but it just wasn't right. Why was she naked and weighted?

He reached for the scotch, the most essential tool in this CSI's box. God how he hated the term Crime Scene Investigator... Crime Scene Imbeciles as far as he was concerned. CSI was a fine example of the corrupting power of television... John was a SOCO not a CSI. A good old fashioned Scenes of Crime Officer who worked away from the limelight using physical evidence to solve crime.

Ben took a large swig of the Coke.

"This is it", he thought, "My dark times are finally over, bring on the light."

The end

4276225R00054

Printed in Great Britain
by Amazon.co.uk, Ltd.,
Marston Gate.